Anthony's Hat

by Deborah Robison

SCHOLASTIC BOOK SERVICES
NEW YORK · TORONTO · LONDON · AUCKLAND · SYDNEY · TOKYO

ISBN: 0-590-00297-x

12 11 10 9 8 7 6 5 4 3   9/7 0 1/8

Printed in the U.S.A   02

For Dennis

Anthony opened his birthday present.

"A new black hat!" he said.

"It's beautiful!"

"I'll go show it to everyone in the neighborhood."

Anthony started down the street.
Plop! A sack of flour
fell off Mrs. Kenny's window sill.

Anthony's hat was covered with flour.

But Anthony didn't know it.

He just kept on walking.

He saw his friend Rosalie sitting on her steps.

"Hey Rosalie!" he said.

"Look at my beautiful black hat."

"That hat is not black," Rosalie said.

"That hat is white."

Anthony smiled.

"I forgot that you don't know your colors yet."

"Oh yes I do," Rosalie said.
Just then, Mr. Albin's red shirt
fell off the clothes line.

"You have a red hat," said Rosalie.

At that very moment, Mrs. Jacobs opened her window.

Out jumped her cat onto the flower box.

The cat made the plants shake.

The green leaves floated down

and piled up on Anthony's hat.

Rosalie said, "You're wearing a green hat."

Anthony said, "No I'm not!
I know what color my own hat is!
This is MY hat and it's BLACK!"

Way up at the top of Rosalie's building,

Mr. Gibson was shaking out his tablecloth.

Oh, no! He shook it a little too hard.

Down

Down

Down it dropped.

It landed very softly on Anthony's hat.

"Now your hat is purple," Rosalie said.

"This is a beautiful BLACK hat! A BLACK HAT!"

Anthony yelled.

"You make me TIRED."

And off he went.

"I'll show it to somebody else."

He turned the corner at the end of the street.
Suddenly — WHOOSH!

The wind blew off the purple tablecloth.
It blew off the green leaves,
the red shirt,
the white flour,
and then it blew off
Anthony's black hat.

"My hat! My hat!
My beautiful black hat!"
Anthony ran and caught it.

"That Rosalie!" he thought.
"She's so little, she hasn't even
learned her colors."

"My goodness," said Rosalie.

She started upstairs for lunch.

"Anthony is a big boy now.

He'd better start learning his colors!"